UPDOG

EXTREME PARKOUR CHALLENGES

Karen Latchana Kenney

Lerner Publications ◆ Minneapolis

Lerner Publications Company
An imprint of Lerner Publishing Group, Inc.
241 First Avenue North
Minneapolis, MN 55401 USA

For reading levels and more information, look up this title at www.lernerbooks.com.

Main body text set in ITC Franklin Gothic Std.
Typeface provided by Adobe Systems.

Editor: Rebecca Higgins **Designer:** Viet Chu

Library of Congress Cataloging-in-Publication Data

Names: Kenney, Karen Latchana, author.
Title: Extreme Parkour challenges / Karen Latchana Kenney.
Description: Minneapolis, MN : Lerner Publications, [2021] | Series: Extreme sports guides (Updog Books) | Includes bibliographical references and index. | Audience: Ages 8–11 | Audience: Grades K–1 | Summary: “Parkour competitions require strength, creativity, and overcoming obstacles. Readers will dive deep into the world of parkour and how athletes face their fears”— Provided by publisher.
Identifiers: LCCN 2020004994 (print) | LCCN 2020004995 (ebook) | ISBN 9781541590441 (library binding) | ISBN 9781728418131 (ebook)
Subjects: LCSH: Parkour—Juvenile literature. | Extreme sports—Juvenile literature.
Classification: LCC GV1068 .K46 2021 (print) | LCC GV1068 (ebook) | DDC 796.42/5—dc23

LC record available at https://lccn.loc.gov/2020004994
LC ebook record available at https://lccn.loc.gov/2020004995

Manufactured in the United States of America
1-47563-48093-6/24/2020

Table of Contents

Urban Athletes

To Damien Walters, a fence isn't just a fence. It's something to land on, jump over, and tumble off.

Walters is an extreme parkour athlete. The city is his playground.

DAMIEN WALTERS

In parkour, athletes use creative moves to get through areas filled with obstacles.

creative: having new or different ideas
obstacle: something that stands in your way

Athletes run, climb, and crawl through difficult courses.

UP NEXT!

Extreme training for parkour.

Parkour Training

Parkour competitions have many kinds of obstacles. Athletes need to train hard to compete.

They train their whole bodies to be strong. They do squats, push-ups, and pull-ups.

squat: an exercise done by crouching close to the ground

Athletes learn parkour moves. Knowing the right moves protects their bodies.

protect: to keep you safe from harm or injury

Athletes train their minds too. They cannot be afraid. They have to trust their bodies and skills.

Bio Break!

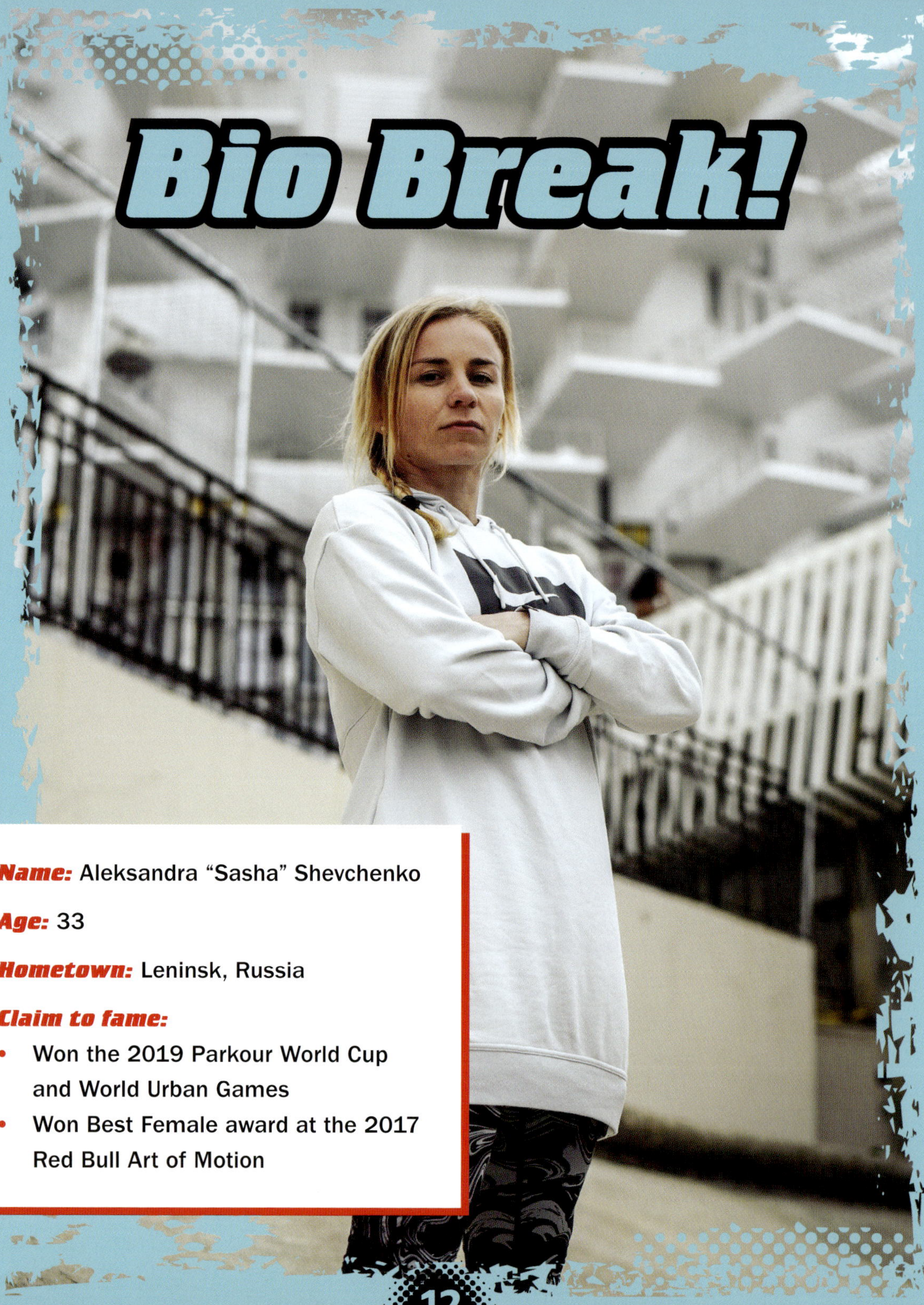

Name: Aleksandra "Sasha" Shevchenko

Age: 33

Hometown: Leninsk, Russia

Claim to fame:

- Won the 2019 Parkour World Cup and World Urban Games
- Won Best Female award at the 2017 Red Bull Art of Motion

SHEVCHENKO COMPETES IN THE 2019 WORLD URBAN GAMES.

Parkour Hacks

- Drink lots of water. Parkour makes you sweat.
- Rest up. Good sleep makes you more alert.
- Start slow. Learn basic moves first. Then work on your speed.
- Do push-ups. Strong arms help you vault.

vault: leap over something using your hands or a pole

For parkour athletes, everywhere is an obstacle course.

UP NEXT!

Parkour's most extreme competitions.

The Biggest Competitions

Athletes test their skills at parkour competitions.

Red Bull Art of Motion takes place on a city course. Athletes jump from roofs and bounce off walls.

The FIG Parkour World Cup has two kinds of events. They are speed-run and freestyle.

freestyle: a competition that does not limit athletes to a certain style

Athletes move fast in speed-run events. They show off difficult moves in freestyle.

In the North American Parkour Championship, athletes race through an indoor course.

Parkour athletes train hard. Only the best athletes get the gold!

Glossary

creative: having new or different ideas

freestyle: a competition that does not limit athletes to a certain style

obstacle: something that stands in your way

protect: to keep you safe from harm or injury

squat: an exercise done by crouching close to the ground

vault: leap over something using your hands or a pole

Check It Out!

American Parkour: The Beginner's Guide to Getting Started in Parkour & Freerunning
http://americanparkour.com/getting-started/

Kenney, Karen Latchana. *Extreme Endurance Challenges.* Minneapolis: Lerner Publications, 2021.

Laughlin, Kara L. *Parkour.* Mankato, MN: Child's World, 2018.

Seeker: Parkour for Beginners
https://www.seeker.com/parkour-for-beginners-5-moves-you-can-master-quickly-1765401410.html

Vescia, Monique. *Extreme Parkour.* New York: Rosen, 2020.

Wonderopolis: What Is Parkour?
https://www.wonderopolis.org/wonder/what-is-parkour

Index

Photo Acknowledgments

Image credits: FotoAndalucia/Shutterstock.com, p. 4; John Lamparski/WireImage/Getty Images, p. 5; DGLimages/Shutterstock.com, p. 6; oneinchpunch/Shutterstock.com, pp. 7, 15; milan2099/Getty Images, p. 8; akturer/Shutterstock.com, p. 9; Reshetnikov_art/Shutterstock.com, p. 10; WAYHOME studio/Shutterstock.com, p. 11; LUCAS BARIOULET/AFP/Getty Images, pp. 12, 18, 19; ATTILA KISBENEDEK/AFP/Getty Images, p. 13; Arsenii Palivoda/Shutterstock.com, p. 16; Predrag Vuckovic/Getty Images, p. 17; iordani/Shutterstock.com, p. 20; Samo Vidic/Getty Images, p. 21. Design elements: rogistok/Shutterstock.com.

Cover image: areporter/Shutterstock.com.